ROCK STAR AND SOFTBOY

completely & utterly by
SINA GRACE

except for lettering by RUS WOOTON

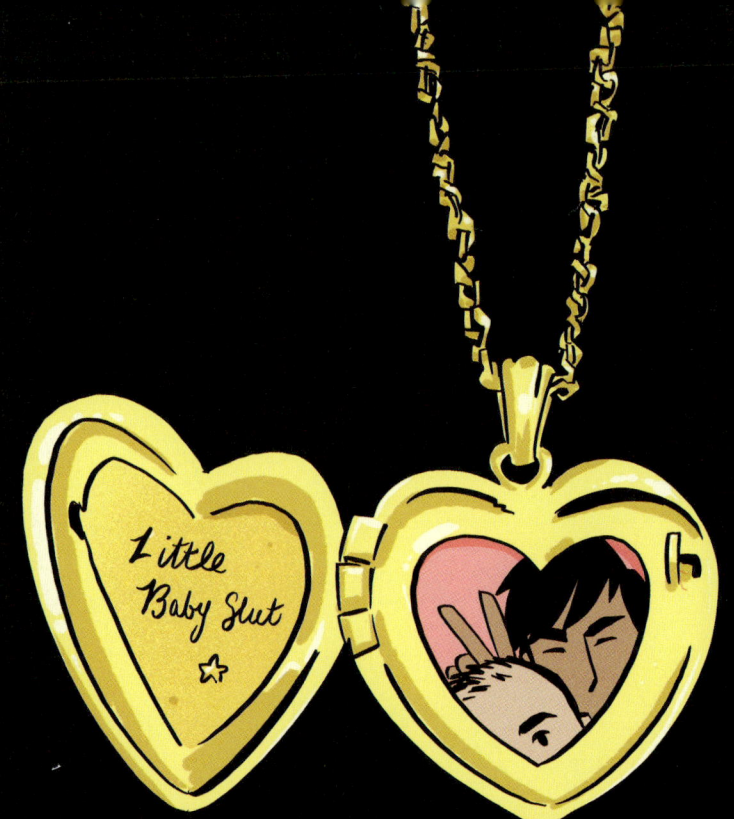

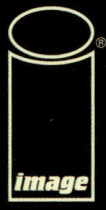

IMAGE COMICS, INC. • **Robert Kirkman**: Chief Operating Officer • **Erik Larsen**: Chief Financial Officer • **Todd McFarlane**: President • **Marc Silvestri**: Chief Executive Officer • **Jim Valentino**: Vice President • **Eric Stephenson**: Publisher / Chief Creative Officer • **Nicole Lapalme**: Controller • **Leanna Caunter**: Accounting Analyst • **Sue Korpela**: Accounting & HR Manager • **Marla Eizik**: Talent Liaison • **Jeff Boison**: Director of Sales & Publishing Planning • **Lorelei Bunjes**: Director of Digital Services • **Dirk Wood**: Director of International Sales & Licensing • **Alex Cox**: Director of Direct Market Sales • **Chloe Ramos**: Book Market & Library Sales Manager • **Emilio Bautista**: Digital Sales Coordinator • **Jon Schlaffman**: Specialty Sales Coordinator • **Kat Salazar**: Director of PR & Marketing • **Drew Fitzgerald**: Marketing Content Associate • **Heather Doornink**: Production Director • **Drew Gill**: Art Director • **Hilary DiLoreto**: Print Manager • **Tricia Ramos**: Traffic Manager • **Melissa Gifford**: Content Manager • **Erika Schnatz**: Senior Production Artist • **Ryan Brewer**: Production Artist • **Deanna Phelps**: Production Artist • IMAGECOMICS.COM

ROCKSTAR AND SOFTBOY (ONE-SHOT). First printing. February 2022. Published by Image Comics, Inc. Office of publication: PO BOX 14457, Portland, OR 97293. Copyright © 2022 Sina Grace. All rights reserved. "Rockstar and Softboy," its logos, and the likenesses of all characters herein are trademarks of Sina Grace, unless otherwise noted. "Image" and the Image Comics logos are registered trademarks of Image Comics, Inc. No part of this publication may be reproduced or transmitted, in any form or by any means (except for short excerpts for journalistic or review purposes), without the express written permission of Sina Grace, or Image Comics, Inc. All names, characters, events, and locales in this publication are entirely fictional. Any resemblance to actual persons (living or dead), events, or places, without satirical intent, is coincidental. Printed in Canada. Representation: Law Offices of Harris M. Miller II, PC (rightsinquiries@gmail.com). ISBN: 978-1-5343-2205-9

DEDICATED TO
JOSH

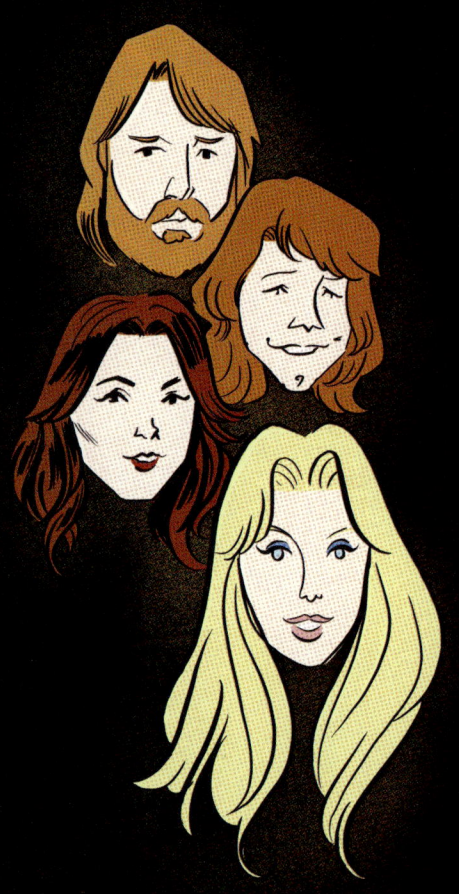
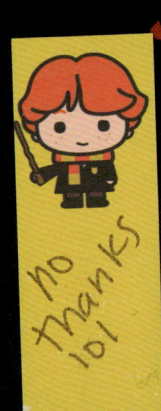

please listen to
ABBA

no thanks lol

while reading

WHAT YOU NEED TO KNOW

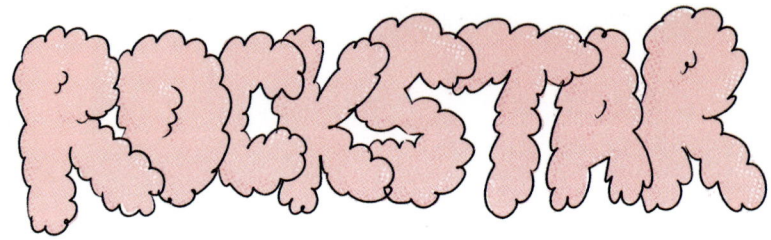

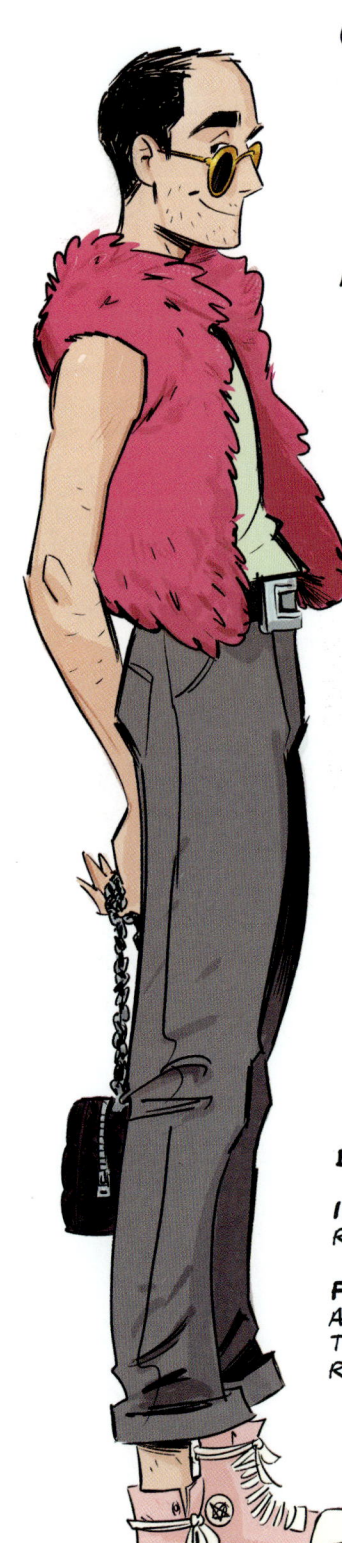

ASTROLOGICAL SIGN: LEO

HEIGHT: 5'10"

BIRTHPLACE: LOS ANGELES, CA

OCCUPATION: TOURING MUSICIAN AND SONGWRITER

FAVORITE STARTER POKÉMON: PIKACHU

HANDBAGS OR HEELS? BOTH!

LIKES: BOYS, MUSIC, CONCERTS, COMIC BOOKS, COLD COFFEE DRINKS, TEQUILA AND WHITE WINE, BODY HAIR, FASHION, THICC BODIES, BOOKS, CASSETTE TAPES

FAVORITE COLOR: MILLENNIAL PINK

LANGUAGES: ENGLISH, FARSI

DISLIKES: COLD FRENCH FRIES, CAVITY BREATH, THE THIRD TRACK ON EVERY SINGLE TAYLOR SWIFT ALBUM

VICES: FUN DRUGS, GUYS WHO SMELL GOOD, SOFT BEARDS, GUCCI

FAVORITE COMIC CHARACTER: SPIDER-MAN, OR THE BIKER DYKES FROM MARS

BOY SMELLS CANDLE OF CHOICE: ITALIAN KUSH

INSPIRATIONS: RAIN ON LEATHER JACKETS, ANY MICK ROCK PHOTO SUBJECT, PATTI SMITH FINGERS

FAVORITE THING ABOUT BFF: THAT HE DOESN'T ACTUALLY LAUGH OUT LOUD, BUT LOOKS LIKE ONE OF THOSE PANDA BEARS EATING BAMBOO WHEN A JOKE REALLY SLAPS.

SOFTBOY

ASTROLOGICAL SIGN: PISCES

HEIGHT: 6'0"

BIRTHPLACE: RIVERSIDE, CA

OCCUPATION: NARRATIVE DESIGNER FOR VIDEO GAMES

FAVORITE STARTER POKÉMON: SQUIRTLE

HANDBAGS OR HEELS? HEELS

LIKES: VINYL RECORDS, PLANTS, WEED, TABLETOP GAMES, RED WINE, REALLY FANCY SKINCARE PRODUCTS, WEEKENDS IN JOSHUA TREE, VIDEO GAMES, MOVIE SOUNDTRACKS, RE-WATCHING THE 'DEATH NOTE' ANIME WHEN SAD

FAVORITE COLOR: BURNT ORANGE

LANGUAGES: ENGLISH, SPANISH

DISLIKES: TARDINESS, MUGGY WEATHER, DOGS THAT DON'T CUDDLE, MAYONNAISE

VICES: GAMING TOO MUCH AND SAYING IT'S FOR WORK, ONLINE SALES, VAPING

FAVORITE COMIC CHARACTER: USAGI (SAILOR MOON)

BOY SMELLS CANDLE OF CHOICE: PHYLLIA

INSPIRATIONS: FURNITURE STORE LOOK BOOKS, DUNGEONS AND DRAGONS MANU-ALS, SOCIAL MEDIA FAMOUS BAKERS

FAVORITE THING ABOUT BFF: HE'LL DROP EVERYTHING TO LISTEN TO ME WHEN I'M HAVING A BAD DAY... LIKE, ONE TIME HE WALKED OUT OF A RECORDING STUDIO AND PAID FOR EVERYONE'S OVERTIME OUT OF HIS OWN POCKET TO BUY US IN-N-OUT AND HEAR ME COMPLAIN ABOUT A WORK FIGHT.

HOW ROCKSTAR AND SOFTBOY MET

Many moons ago, Rockstar ended up at a lackluster ABBA tribute show because he thought the "Benny" was hot.

To the corner of his eye, he saw Softboy at the bar alone, wearing a handmade *VOYAGE** shirt.

*THE KINDA MEH BUT VERY GLAD-IT-EXISTS ABBA REUNION ALBUM.

Rockstar loved that someone else appreciated the custody battle disco banger "Keep an Eye on Dan" as much as him...

...so much so that he decided to **TAKE A CHANCE** on a stranger at a gig and strike up a conversation.

The pair became inseparable ever since.

They did everything together, even volunteering to rid the city of its pesky Tibetan Torgul demon infestation!

Rockstar and Softboy weren't just supportive, they made each other **BETTER**.

SO HERE WE ARE TODAY, WITH **TWO BEST FRIENDS**, LIVING TOGETHER IN HOLLYWEIRD, MAKING DREAMS COME TRUE ON FEVERISH BLVD.

THEY SPEND THEIR DAYS NOURISHING ONE ANOTHER'S CREATIVITY--SOFTBOY HELPING ROCKSTAR COME UP WITH WITTY LYRICS TO SONGS AND ROCKSTAR BEING A SOUNDING BOARD FOR THE VARIOUS GAMES SOFTBOY WORKS ON.

WHILE THEY DON'T NECESSARILY AGREE ON EVERYTHING (ROCKSTAR WILL NEVER WATCH AN ANIME BUT TAKES UP TOO MUCH SHELF SPACE WITH HIS MANGA COLLECTION), THEIR SITUATION AS ROOMMATES AND BEST FRIENDS IS AS PERFECT AS **ANYONE** COULD EVER HOPE FOR.

EVER.

HUH. INFORMATIVE.
OKAY, BUT THE TOAD NEEDS A CHALLENGE THERE...
...I COULD BRING STELLA SNAIL INTO THAT CHAPTER, BUT DOES THAT AFFECT THOSE TWO TREES?
HEY, SOFTBOY, WHAT'S WITH THE MURDER MYSTERY WALL?
SETH?!
IT'S A FLOWCHART FOR A NEW IDEA I'M WORKING ON... A NEW NARRATIVE GAME.
WHAT ARE YOU DOING IN MY HOUSE-- AT 8AM?
OH, YOUR ROOMMATE HAD ME, UHH... **OVER** LAST NIGHT.

WHY DON'T YOU JUST USE AN EXCEL SHEET FOR THIS STUFF?
IT HELPS ME TO VISUALIZE THE STORY SEEING ALL THE CHOICES PLAY OUT BIG IN FRONT OF ME.
DO YOU KNOW WHERE ROCKSTAR IS? I WOKE UP, AND HE WASN'T AROUND.
BASED ON THE THRUM OF HEELS APPROACHING THE FRONT DOOR, I'D SAY HE'S COMING BACK IN RIGHT ABOUT--
GL BICH
LOOK WHAT THE CAT DRAGGED IN--
--ME! WITH COFFEE FOR ALL!
OH SHIT, I'M GONNA MISS THE SQUIRRELS EATING ON A LITTLE PICNIC TABLE!
LOOK, ROCKSTAR, IT'S MY OLD CO-WORKER, WEARING LONG JOHNS IN OUR LIVING ROOM.

S'CUTE, RIGHT?
YEP. BEST THING TO SEE ON A SATURDAY.
I MEAN, WHY DISCRIMINATE TO JUST SATURDAYS ONLY, LONG JOHNS ARE EVERGREEN CUTE IF YOU ASK--
--OH.
SORRY TO SEND YOU OFF SO SOON IN THE MORNING, BUT TODAY'S OUR VERY SPECIAL BFF DAY OF THE WEEK.
YOU UNDERSTAND, DON'T YOU?
SURE, I'LL SKIDADDLE.
HE'S GATHERING HIS THINGS, I'LL TAKE A QUICK RINSE, AND WE CAN GET RIGHT TO BUSINESS!
SO TURN YOUR CURMUDGEON BROWS UPSIDE DOWN!
ROCKSTAR.
YOU HOOKED UP WITH SETH?!
MY CO-WORKER?!
IT COULD GET SO AWKWARD IF YOU TWO START DATING OR HAVE A BAD BREAK-UP!
OKAY, FIRSTLY--YOU FREELANCED TOGETHER AT A GAME COMPANY THREE MONTHS AGO. YOU'RE COLLEAGUES, NOT CO-WORKERS.
AND SECONDLY--
--SETH'S A FULL-TIME BOTTOM AND A VIRGO.
YOU KNOW I NEED THE FULL SEXUAL MENU AND ASTROLOGICAL COMPATIBILITY FOR ROMANCE.
NOW STOP COMING UP WITH WORST-CASE-SCENARIO NARRATIVES AND GIVE ME SOME POSI VIBES...

"...WE'VE GOT A FULL DAY AHEAD."
I'M JUST SAYING...
MY FRIEND BIJ STARTED A FOOT ACCOUNT THIS YEAR AND ALREADY HAS MORE FOLLOWERS THAN ME.
PEOPLE PAY HIM LITERALLY HUNDREDS OF DOLLARS TO SEND OVER SOCKS HE'S JIZZED ON.
IT WOULD TAKE A LOT OF PRESSURE OFF THIS GAME YOU'RE CREATING FROM SCRATCH IF YOU HAD A LITTLE FOOT FETISH SIDE HUSTLE.
I DON'T NEED A FOOT FETISH ACCOUNT TO SUBSIDIZE MY VIDEO GAME. SAVINGS FROM ROYALTIES ON HALF YOUR SONGS IS ENOUGH.
NOW, CAN YOU FOCUS AND HELP ME WITH THIS NEW CHARACTER?
NO BUT REALLY, @FEETPRAYLOVE WOULD TAKE SOCIAL MEDIA BY STORM.
IF WE PUT THESE TUSSIES ONLINE, YOU COULD FIND TRUE LOVE'S KISS.
FOCUS.
OKAY... MAJA MAPLE, WHO EVEN IS SHE???
SHE'S A CARAMEL-COLORED ARMADILLO.
SHE OWNS A BAKERY NEXT TO TOADAL FITNESS. BUNDTERCOVER CAKES?
SHE'S CLASSY. HUMBLE. LIVES FOR A CLASSIC PEARL NECKLACE.
WHEN'S THE LAST TIME YOU HAD A DATE, ANYWAY?

I DONNO... LIKE NINE MONTHS?
I'VE BEEN BUSY FOCUSING ON GETTING MATERIALS READY FOR THIS GAME'S KICKSTARTER.
NINE MONTHS WITHOUT SO MUCH AS EVEN A BLOWIE OR A HANDY-JO?!
IF YOU WERE ACE, THAT WOULD BE FINE--BUT YOU'RE JUST AS MUCH OF A SLAG AS ME, SO THIS IS A PROBLEM.
NO WONDER THIS GAME'S LIKE PULLING TEETH--YOU NEED TO GET PLOWED!
LIKE, DEEPLY DICKED BY A DONG THAT FUCKS THE INSPIRATION IN YOUR GUTS BACK UP TO THAT BEAUTIFUL BRAIN OF YOURS!
WELL, I GUESS WE'RE DONE WORKING FOR THE DAY.
SO WHAT, SHOULD WE THROW A SEX PARTY AND IT'LL SOLVE MY CREATIVE BLOCKAGE?
THAT'S IT!
A PARTY--NOT LIKE AN ORGY, BUT AN ACTUAL RAGER!

THINK ABOUT IT--
WE INVITE A **BUNCH** OF PEOPLE FROM DIFFERENT SOCIAL CIRCLES TO OUR HOUSE PARTY.
BETWEEN THE TWO OF US, THERE'LL BE A POTENTIAL NEW LOVER TO DO THINGS TO YOUR BODY.
AND WORSE COMES TO WORST-- WE'LL MAKE **NEW** MEMORIES AND HAVE A BLAST!
A **PARTY?!** I'LL MAKE DIP.
SEE? **MIAOW MIAOW'S** IN.
SHE DOESN'T ACTUALLY LIVE HERE.
THAT'S JUST GONNA BE A ***DISTRACTION,*** AND I'LL PROBABLY BE LEFT WITH CLEANING ALL THE DISHES UP.
WHY ARE YOU NEGGING ON THE IDEA?
THIS IS THE ***PERFECT*** HOUSE FOR A PARTY... HAVE YOU GUYS EVEN THROWN ONE SINCE YOU MOVED IN?!
HMMMMM.

LET ME THINK ON IT... LATER. I NEED TO PREP FOR D&D TONIGHT.
I DID NOT COMMIT TO YOUR SCHEME YET!
YES! WE'RE HAVING A PARTY AND GETTING MY BABY LAID!
AND QUIT LIGHTING CANCER STICKS IN THE HOUSE, MIAOW MIAOW!
I'M MYTHICAL, I CAN'T GET CANCER.
BUT THE REST OF US CAN!
WHAT ARE YOU GONNA DO TO CONVINCE HIM TO SAY YES?
OH PLEASE, I DON'T HAVE TO DO ANYTHING. HE'S GONNA SAY YES BY TOMORROW MORNING.

I KNOW HOW SOFTBOY'S GORGEOUS NOGGIN WORKS, HE'LL COME TO THE DECISION ON HIS OWN.
IN FACT--
--I'D GO AS FAR AS BETTING TWENTY WHOLE DOLLARS THAT THINGS WILL GO DOWN EXACTLY AS FOLLOWS...
"...WHILE SOFTBOY PLAYS DUNGEON MASTER FOR HIS GROUP, HIS MIND WILL WANDER INTO **FOMO** TERRITORY.
"HE'LL BE DM TO ***HIS OWN LIFE,*** CREATING DIFFERENT SCENARIOS ABOUT EVERYTHING THAT WON'T HAPPEN IN HIS LIFE IF HE SAYS NO TO OPPORTUNITY.
"THE POTENTIAL OF FOMO WILL WEIGH HIM DOWN SO MUCH THAT HE'LL WANT TO MAKE THE PARTY SEEM LIKE **HIS** IDEA BY MORNING.
"AND WHILE SOFTBOY IS GOING THROUGH THAT WHOLE JOURNEY, I WILL BE MAKING BEDROOM EYES AT A HANDSOME GENTLEMAN WHOSE DMs I SLID INTO THIS WEEK."
I'M DOING **MY** PART IN PROPHECY FULFILLMENT BY ASKING SAID GENT OUT TO AKBAR IN A FEW HOURS!

THE NEXT MORNING.
ROCKSTAR. ROCKSTAR!
I STUDIED, I SWEAR!
YEESH, WHAT HAPPENED TO YOU LAST NIGHT?
I THOUGHT MY FRIEND WAS GIVING ME A BUMP OF COKE TO PEP ME UP AT THE BAR... IT WAS KETAMINE.
I HATE KETAMINE--IT ALWAYS FEELS LIKE I'M IN THAT ORGY MUSIC VIDEO FOR "STITCHES."*
*VERY DEEP CUT, BUT IYKYK. --ED.
YOU SAID THAT THE LAST TIME YOU "ACCIDENTALLY" DID KETAMINE.
WELL, MAYBE THIS WILL CHEER YOU UP...
...I THINK WE SHOULD THROW A HOUSE PARTY.
SARAH YESSICA PARKER!
I'VE PICKED UP A FEW BOOKS ON HISTORICALLY GREAT PARTIES, AND WHAT WE CAN DO TO MAKE THIS ONE THE MOST EFFECTIVE FOR--
BABE, I'M LITERALLY ONE STEP AHEAD OF YOU. LEMME FIND MY IPAD...

YEP, GOOD-- WASN'T A KETAMINE DREAM.
I'VE MADE A DRAFT OF WHAT WE NEED TO THROW A GOOD TIME FOR OUR GUESTS.
BEHOLD!
PERFECT PARTY
photo opp + polaroidz
Bevs & Snacks
spiked punch
(grab 5 sprigs o' sixfoil, figs ash, pinecone oil + a drop o' feverfew)
(+ candy!!)
H2O
Charged Crystals
(carnelian + juniper)
MUSIC!
(outdoor DJ?!)
karaoke (separate room)
fire pit
2 bad bitchez
duh
ACTIVITIES
tarot
Bart Simpson
good scents
fog/mist machine
(or a spell?)
free drugs!
pre-smudged home
NO DRUGS.
THIS IS FAIRLY COMPREHENSIVE... NOW WE HAVE TO FIGURE OUT WHO TO INVITE.
OKAY, CONSIDER ME TWO STEPS AHEAD OF YOU!

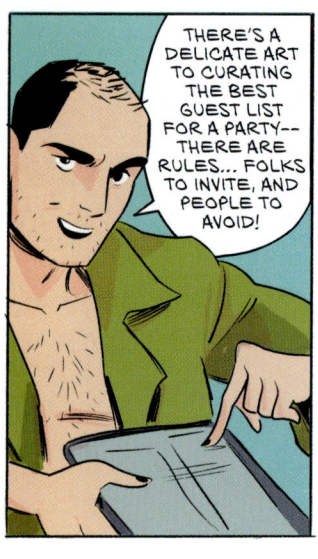

There's a delicate art to curating the best guest list for a party—there are rules... folks to invite, and people to avoid!

Rule 1: CAST A WIDE AND DIVERSE NET!

The **BEST THINGS** happen when people from **DIFFERENT GROUPS** meet for the first time! Invite from all different social circles!

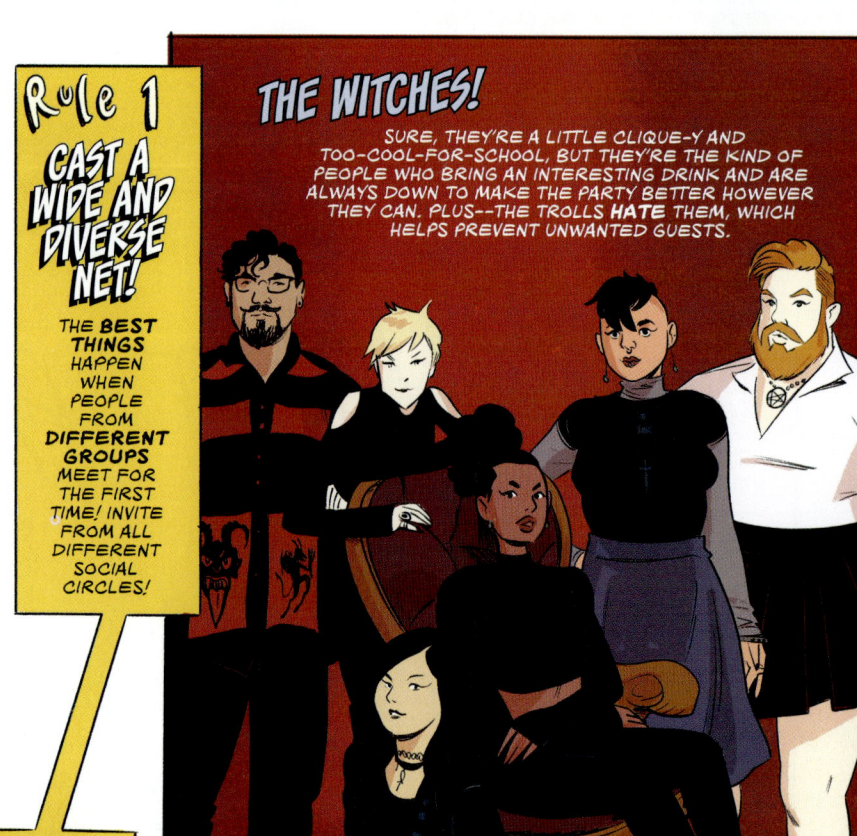

THE WITCHES!

Sure, they're a little clique-y and too-cool-for-school, but they're the kind of people who bring an interesting drink and are always down to make the party better however they can. Plus—the trolls **HATE** them, which helps prevent unwanted guests.

Rule 2: OVER-INVITE BY A LOT!

Having bodies in the house is one of the key things we need to start a vibe. It sounds stressful, but if we want 50 people to show up, we should invite **DOUBLE** that. No-shows abound!

THE ZOMBIES!

Okay, I think these fools get a bad rap. For how slow they are to move, they usually show up on time and leave early, they bring their own bevs... and at worst, they just chew the scenery.

Rule 3 KNOW YOUR VIBE!
KNOWING WHAT KIND OF PARTY YOU WANT TO HAVE WILL DICTATE HOW MANY OF ANY GROUP TO INVITE. EXAMPLE: TOO MANY GAMERS, AND EVERYONE'S PLAYING MARIO KART BY 10:30.
THE VAMPIRES
THEY SHOW UP LATE (ALWAYS), AND TEND TO BE DRAINING... BUT A FEW VAMPS WILL HELP MAKE THINGS A LITTLE SEXY.
Rule 4 MAKE IT WEIRD!
WEIRDOS ARE A GREAT THING! THEY PUT SQUARES OUT OF THEIR COMFORT ZONE AND PUSH THINGS TOWARDS ARTY GOOD TIME.
THE FAERIES!
THEY'LL NEVER RSVP, THEY'LL PROBABLY TRACK MUD IN THE HOUSE, BUT THESE INCONSISTENT BABES KNOW THE FUCKING VIBES. JUST BE READY FOR ONE OR THREE OF THEM TO PASS OUT ON A COUCH.
Rule 5-ish THE X-FACTOR!
INVITE ONE PERSON WHO CAN POTENTIALLY MAKE THINGS DANGEROUS...
SORCERER STU!
THEY HAVE A DRUG, SPELL, AND CHARM FOR ANY OCCASION. NO ONE NEEDS TO KNOW THEY MAKE THE POTIONS IN THEIR MOM'S CRAFT ROOM.
LET'S HAVE THE PARTY ON A FULL MOON-- EVERYTHING WILL BE CHARGED TO ELEVEN FOR A GREAT TIME.
YAY US.
WAIT.
FULL MOON. SIXFOIL. WITCHES. VAMPIRES. DRUGGIE SORCERER...
...I SAW SOMETHING ABOUT THOSE ELEMENTS.
THERE--

THERE'S A RITUAL, DATING BACK TO THE 16TH CENTURY, THAT COULD BRING ABOUT--
--THE PARTY ANIMAL.
PVRTY AN
A MISCHIEF DEMON WHO SEEMS LIKE BACCHUS GOT FISTED BY BEETLEJUICE, THE PARTY ANIMAL CONSUMES CHAOS, AND THERE'S NO RECORD OF HOW TO GET RID OF IT ONCE SUMMONED.
INVITING THE WITCHES AND SORCERER STU... ONE OF THEM COULD HAVE THE RIGHT AMULET NEEDED TO TRIGGER A SUMMONING SPELL WITH EVERYTHING ELSE WE HAVE IN THE HOUSE--

BORING.
THE PARTY ANIMAL IS A GODDAMN URBAN LEGEND TOLD TO SCARE KIDS FROM TRYING TO CHARM THEIR KEGS.
WE NEED THE WITCHES, THE MOON, THE PUNCH AND SORCERER STU.
YOU HAVING A SEXY MAGICAL NIGHT IS MORE IMPORTANT THAN WORRYING ABOUT A MADE-UP MUSKRAT, OR GOAT, OR WHATEVER IT IS.
CAN WE AT LEAST TELL THE WITCHES AND STU TO NOT BRING ANY PERSONAL EFFECTS?
THAT'S LIKE CELESTIAL PROFILING-- NO WAY.
OOH! I'M BEAUTIFUL-MINDING SOME MORE IDEAS...
...LET'S FINISH PARTY PLANNING OVER EGGS AND BREAKFAST POTATOES AT LITTLE DOM'S.
THIS PARTY IS GONNA BE THE BEST!

AND JUST LIKE THAT... PEOPLE ALL AROUND LOS ANGELES GOT INVITED TO ROCKSTAR AND SOFTBOY'S HOUSE PARTY.
you're invited
Please join us for a
DANK HOUSE PARTY
honoring this thing called
L I F E
Saturday, Feb 12th, 8:00 pm
321 Feverish Blvd | LA, CA
Hosted by your faves, Rockstar and Softboy
No regrets! C U there
(No gifts, either)
friends first
DID YOU GET A LOCKET AND ROSE PETALS IN YOUR INVITE, TOO?
I HAVEN'T SEEN THOSE GUYS SINCE OUR BOOK CLUB DISBANDED, SO I AM WILLING TO MOVE OUR SACRIFICE TO EARLIER IN THE DAY.
I DON'T HAVE A PROBLEM WITH THAT.
I'LL LET THE ECHO PARK COVEN KNOW WE'RE GOING!
GREAT!

YOU DON'T REALLY NEED TO **SEE** THE DAYS LEADING UP TO THE PARTY.

ROCKSTAR AND SOFTBOY DELEGATED TASKS BASED ON THEIR RESPECTIVE STRENGTHS TO AVOID **FRICTION**.

ROCKSTAR'S MOM VISITED A FEW TIMES AND BROUGHT **HOMEMADE PERSIAN FOOD** OVER TO KEEP THE BOYS **HEALTHY**.

MIAOW MIAOW **PISSED** ON SOFTBOY'S CHEST WHILE HE WAS SLEEPING WHEN HE TRIED TO SWITCH HER LITTER WITH THOSE WEIRD **PELLET** THINGS.

SOFTBOY ADDED MORE POST-ITS OF STORY BEATS FOR HIS GAME... YET SOMEHOW MADE NO MAJOR PROGRESS.

THE DAY OF THE PARTY.

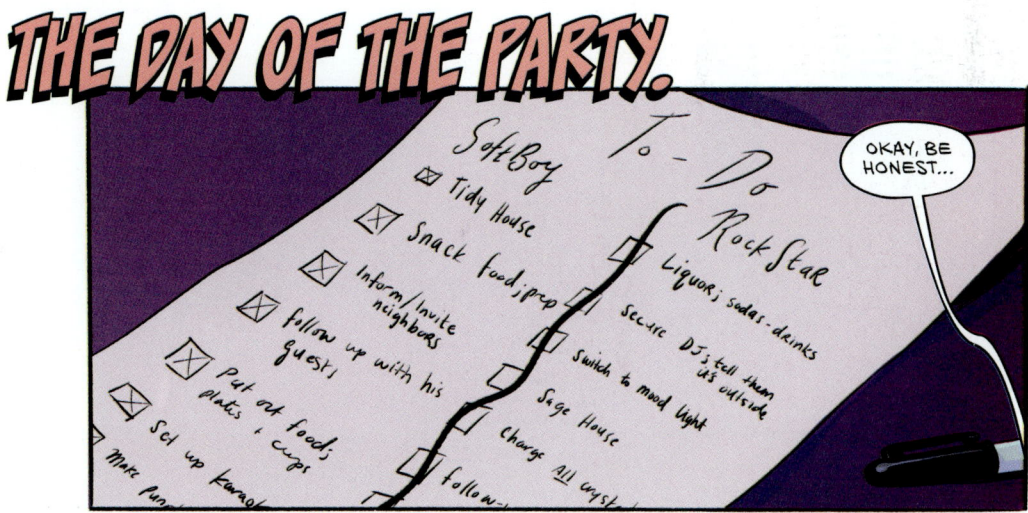

"OKAY, BE HONEST..."

HOW DO I LOOK?
UHHM, HELLO, CHEST! I'M LOVING THIS LIKE SLUTTY NORMCORE MOMENT YOU'RE HAVING!
ALRIGHT, ALRIGHT. YOU LOOK GREAT, TOO.

UHH, WHY IS SETH ASKING IF I'M FREE TO PLAY SETTLERS OF CATAN TONIGHT, ROCKSTAR?
THE GLASSES-- TOO MUCH, OR JUST ENOUGH?
ROCKSTAR... DID YOU NOT INVITE SETH?
YOU'RE RIGHT, I LOOK LIKE A MEGAMAN VILLAIN IN THEM.
AND YES, UNWRITTEN RULE ABOUT PARTIES--DON'T INVITE HOOK-UPS YOU DON'T WANT TO HOOK UP WITH!
SEE?! HOOKING UP WITH HIM MADE THINGS MESSY!
HE'S GONNA FIND SOMETHING ABOUT THIS PARTY ON SOCIAL MEDIA AND FEEL LEFT OUT.
DING-DONG!
BATHROOM IS THAT DOOR
OH MY GOD, YOU'RE LITERALLY JUST LOOKING FOR SOMETHING TO GET UPSET ABOUT, 'CUZ TONIGHT'S GONNA BE PERFECT.
WATCH...
HEY, GUYS, SORRY WE'RE A FEW MINUTES LATE. TRAFFIC ON THE 405 WAS NUTS!
LUCKILY THE GAS STATION HAD SOME DECENT BEERS!
ZOMBIES ON TIME TO THE PARTY, WITH WARM PBR.
CALLED IT.

A FEW HOURS LATER, NOT A HITCH NOR A PROBLEM IN SIGHT.
WOW. PEOPLE REALLY LOVE SHITTY POLAROIDS...
OF COURSE THEY DO, MIAOW MIAOW. EVERYTHING IS PERFECT.
LIKE, ABBA-SOLUTELY EVERYTHING.
EVEN OUR SWEET ANGEL IS FLIRTING WITH SOMEONE WHO LOOKS LIKE A C-LIST X-MEN CHARACTER.*
*IF SOFTBOY HAD A TYPE, IT WOULD BE JUST THAT. --ED.
THIS DAMN FOG MACHINE CANNOT FIND A BALANCE THOUGH... I WANT A DANCE FLOOR MOOD, NOT A JOHN CARPENTER MOVIE!
CHECK AND SEE IF PEOPLE ARE EATING MY DIP, I NEED A CIG!
ALRIGHT, IF A HINKY FOG MACHINE IS MY BIGGEST PROBLEM, I'LL GLADLY TAKE IT--
--HUH?!

(WHILE SOME KIND OF DANCE-Y DOJA CAT SONG WAS ACTUALLY PLAYING, ALL ROCKSTAR COULD HEAR IN HIS HEAD WAS ORVILLE PECK'S "DEAD OF NIGHT," FOR OBVIOUS REASONS.
HE'S SO...
...QUTE-- WITH A CAPITAL Q!

OH, HEY--
--YOU'RE ROCKSTAR. THIS IS YOUR PLACE, RIGHT?!
MY FRIENDS DINO AND JESSE* BROUGHT ME ALONG. THIS PARTY'S GREAT!
THANKS, WE THREW IT TOGETHER LAST MINUTE.
*GOD BLESS THE FAERIES.
THERE'S ACTUALLY A DJ SPINNING VINYL IN THE BACKYARD, IF YOU WANNA CHECK IT OUT.
THE BACK-YARD IS JUST OVER THIS WAY--
DID YOU SEE THEIR DISH-WASHER!?
KENMORE MAKES THE BEST DISHWASHERS. MINE IS A COMPLETE LIFESAVER.
ACTUALLY, GIVE ME ONE SECOND!

SORCERER STU!
PEOPLE ARE TALKING ABOUT APPLIANCES! THIS PARTY COULD BE VEERING TO SNOOZE TOWN, AND I'M GONNA BE TOO DISTRACTED TO MAKE SURE THINGS STAY FUN!
SAY NO MORE BABES, I GOT YOU COVERED.
GO DO ROCKSTAR THINGS, THIS AMULET'S CARRYING VIBES FROM BEYONCÉ'S COACHELLA PERFORMANCE...
...AND I'VE BEEN WAITING FOR THE PERFECT OCCASION TO UNLEASH IT.
HEY EVERYONE-- I JUST GOT A NOSE RING!
WHOA, LOOKS LIKE THE KARAOKE MACHINE IS ONLY ALLOWING SPICE GIRLS SONGS!
HONESTLY, WERK!
DID AN ICE CREAM TRUCK JUST PULL UP!?

SO ANYWAY... WHERE WERE WE?
IT'S TIME TO LIVE--
LAUGH--
AND GET **LOADED!**
DID YOU SEE THAT FLASH OF LIGHT?
WHUZZAT?

LOOKIE WHAT CAME WITH ME-- DRUGS!
WHO WANTS A FENTANYL LOLLIPOP!?
I LOVE A CHICK WHO DOESN'T WEAR A BRA!
HISSSSS!
KRASH!
THAT SOUNDS LIKE CERAMIC.
AWW, MAN, I REALLY NEEDED TO MAKE A SISSY--
--WHAT'S THIS?
WHO LIT THE ENCHANTED PUNCH ON FIRE?
WHERE IS ROCKSTAR--
--OH GOD NO.
ART, MAN.
IT CAN MEAN ANYTHING, REALLY.

OOWWWOOOOOOOOOOOOOOOOOOOOOOOOO
ROCKSTAR!
YOU DID THIS--AND I TOLD YOU IT WOULD HAPPEN!
THE PARTY ANIMAL SHOWED UP, SMASHED MY SUCCULENTS, AND RUINED MY GAME BOARD!
I SHOULD HAVE NEVER LISTENED TO YOUR SELFISH SCHEME TO GET YOURSELF LAID!
I'VE ONLY BEEN TRYING TO GET YOU LAID!
SO I COULD HELP YOU WITH THAT STUPID GAME THAT'S NEVER GOING TO COME TOGETHER!
BUT FINE, PIN EVERY BAD THING THAT HAPPENS TO YOU ON ME. FORGET ABOUT ALL THE GOOD I'VE DONE!
ALL YOU'RE GOOD FOR IS USING PEOPLE WHO CAN BENEFIT YOUR EGO, CAREER, OR COCK!
THAT'S WHAT WE ALL ARE TO YOU--PEOPLE TO KISS YOUR ASS OR SUCK YOUR DICK!
SO DON'T EVEN TRY IT--WITH YOUR THREE GUITAR CHORDS AND UGLY CLOTHES, ACTING LIKE YOU'D HAVE A CAREER WITHOUT ME TO MILK LYRICS FROM!
I...

MY CLOTHES ARE **NOT** UGLY! YOU'RE JUST JEALOUS BECAUSE SHIRLEY KURATA WOULDN'T STYLE YOU FOR ZOE KRAVITZ'S HALF-BIRTHDAY!
I THINK OUR COVEN IS HITTING PRECINCT FOR A DRAG SHOW IF Y'ALL WANNA JOIN UP.
WAIT-- YOU GUYS CAN'T **LEAVE** YET!
IT'S NOT EVEN MIDNIGHT!
DON'T FORGET TO HASHTAG **#ROCKSTARANDSOFTBOY** ON PICS FROM THE NIGHT!
GREAT. EVERYONE'S **GONE.**
ARE YOU **HAPPY** NOW?!
OR DO YOU NEED TO KEEP LAYING INTO ME, EVEN WITHOUT AN--

--AUDIENCE?
YEAH, SOFTBOY'S GONE.
HE JUST...
...LEFT?
WE DIDN'T FINISH FIGHTING THO'. WE'RE STILL IN A FIGHT. AND HE'S GONE...

"...WHERE DID HE GO?"

I KNOW THIS IS REALLY MESSED UP, GIVEN THAT WE DIDN'T INVITE YOU TO THE PARTY, BUT...
...WE JUST HAD A HUGE FIGHT, AND I DIDN'T KNOW WHERE ELSE TO GO.
320
IT'S ALL GOOD. I ENDED UP ORDERING PIZZA AND PLAYING FORTNITE.
COME ON IN.

THE NEXT DAY, ERR--NIGHT.
GET UP.
YOU ALREADY RUINED MY AFTERNOON NAP SLEEPING ON THAT BEANBAG.
GET UP NOW.
LEAVE ME ALONE. I'M WALLOWING.
YEAH, BUT YOU'VE BEEN WALLOWING FOR LIKE **NINE HOURS** STRAIGHT. YOU SMELL LIKE A BURRITO THAT'S BEEN SITTING IN A GYM BAG.
GET UP!
NO. I LOST MY BEST FRIEND, 'CUZ I'M A **MONSTER.**
I'M THE PARTY ANIMAL.
YOU GUYS ARE SO MELODRAMATIC.
AUGH-- LAY OFF!
LISTEN TO ME!
LOOK, I'VE BEEN ALIVE SEVEN HUNDRED YEARS, I'VE **SEEN** SOME SHIT.
LOTS OF FRIEND FIGHTS.
ELLA FITZGERALD FORGAVE MARILYN MONROE FOR STRETCHING HER BRAS.
TOLKIEN GOT OVER C.S. LEWIS'S RELIGIOUS TALK.
JUST SAY SORRY, AND YOU'LL OVERCOME.
PLUS, THE **ACTUAL** PARTY ANIMAL IS FUCKING SOME EVENT UP DOWNTOWN.
SO... YOU SHOULD MAYBE GO **FIX** THAT.

CAN'T LET THE PARTY ANIMAL RUIN ANY MORE LIVES OR FRIENDSHIPS. **WON'T** LET HIM--
OH. **HEY.**
I SAW ON INSTAGRAM STORIES THAT A COYOTE WAS RUINING KENDALL JENNER'S GRAIN-FREE OAT MILK LAUNCH PARTY.
SOFTBOY, I'M **SORRY** FOR EVERYTHING. YOU WERE RIGHT!
MY ACTIONS ARE MOSTLY ALWAYS SELFISH, AND I **HATE** THAT YOU THINK I'M USING YOU, BECAUSE--
NO, ROCKSTAR... **PLEASE.**
I'VE BEEN CRASHING AT SETH'S... AND HE WATCHED PORN IN FRONT OF ME LAST NIGHT, THEN TRIED TO GET ME IN A THREESOME TONIGHT.
I WISH I COULD PUT INTO WORDS HOW **SPECIAL** IT IS TO LOVE ANOTHER MAN THIS MUCH WITHOUT ROMANCE OR SEX ON THE TABLE.
THERE'S NEVER BEEN THAT BETWEEN **US**--NO ULTERIOR MOTIVE, NO WEIRD VIBES.
YOU WANTED TO BE MY FRIEND TO HAVE A FRIEND-- THERE'S **NOTHING** PURER THAN THAT.
SURE, I NEED TO STAND UP FOR MYSELF MORE OFTEN AND SAY "NO" TO YOU, BUT THAT'S **MY** JOURNEY-- NOT YOURS.
I'M SORRY I BLEW UP AT THE PARTY.
BABE, I'M LIKE LITERALLY GONNA CRY, BUT I THINK WE HAVE TO KILL THE PARTY ANIMAL.
GOD, WHEN'S THE LAST TIME WE'VE DONE THIS?
WHEN WE VANQUISHED THAT AWFUL BANSHEE TWO ROWS BEHIND US AT THE CELINE DION CONCERT.
READY...?

I CALL ON THE POWER OF BEING TURBO GAY!
The Suits! The weapons! An ode to Sailor Moon and He-Man! I LOVE THIS! Okay - powerrangers too - but I never watched that show.
©'21 SANRIO

HAIM SABAN, EAT YOUR HEART OUT.

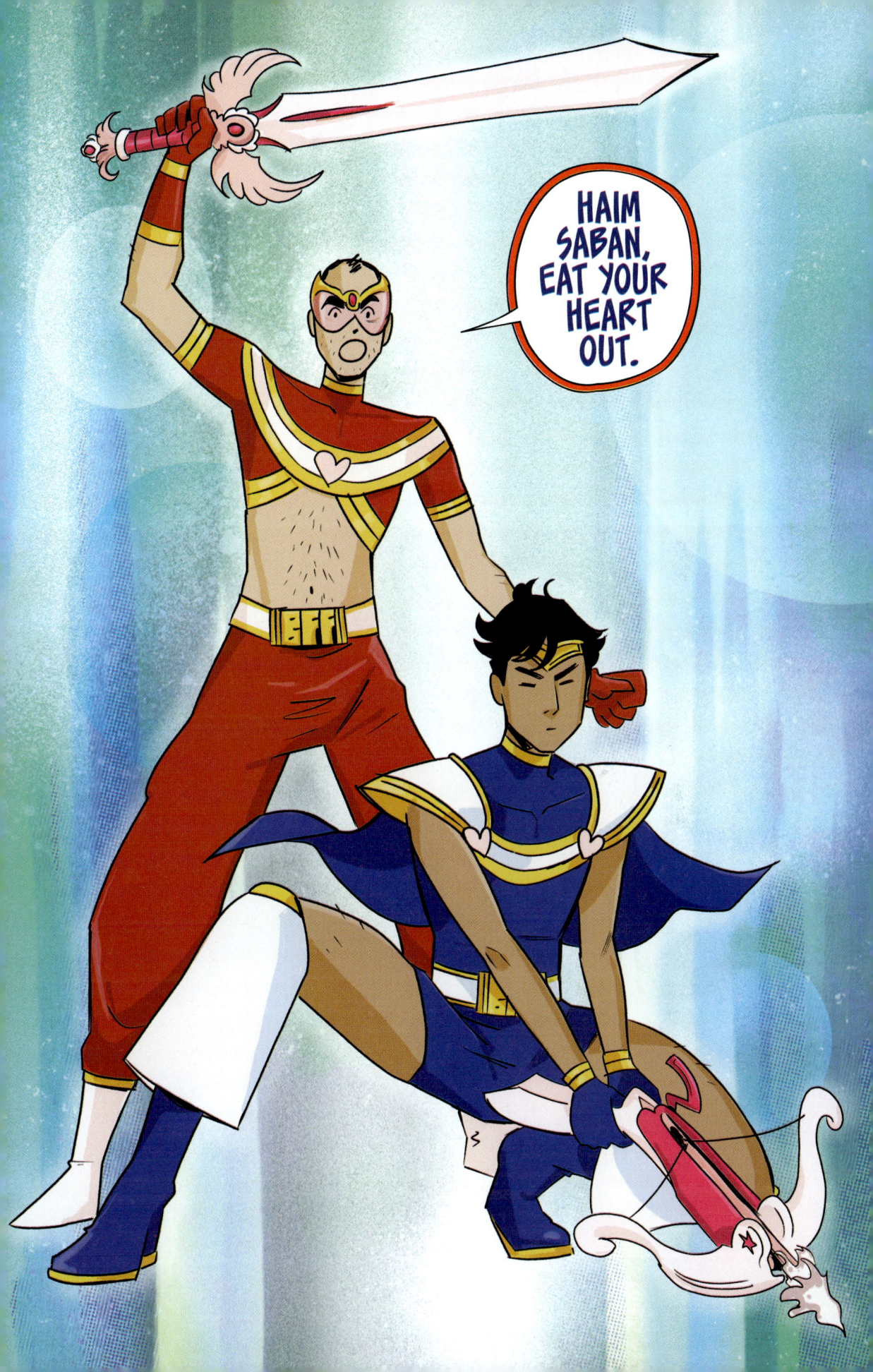

HOW DO YOU FEEL ABOUT SKIPPING THE SMALL TALK AND JUMPING RIGHT INTO THE **MEGA BLAST** PORTION OF THE EVENING?
IF WE MAKE IT BACK HOME IN THE NEXT THIRTY MINUTES, WE CAN SQUEEZE IN TWO EPISODES OF *REAL HOUSEWIVES.*
I'LL EVEN LET YOU PUT ON POTOMAC.*
EXCELLENT!
*CAN WE ALL ADMIT THAT THE PARTY ANIMAL IS A BROKEN WHORE FROM HAMPTON UNIVERSITY? --ED.
HEY, **YOU!**
ALSO, WHAT THE HELL **IS** THIS PARTY? COUCHES AND A DJ BOOTH IN A WHITE WAREHOUSE-- WHERE'S THE **VISION,** THE ELEGAN--
FOCUS, ROCKSTAR.
OKAY, RIGHT...
BRA-ZIIIIING!
...PARTY'S OVER!

Acknowledgments

Thank you to my sisters Stephanie, Detra, and Tamaqua for encouraging me to own my beauty through authorship.

Thank you to my beautiful baby girl: You are my heart and inspiration. May you always know that you are God's masterpiece.

HE'S GONE!

WE DID IT!

WAIT... WHY IS THE RUBBLE MOVING?

OOOOWWWWOOOOOOO!

THAT WAS A ZESTY SOUND BATH!

IT DIDN'T WORK.

WE ONLY MADE HIM STRONGER.

BRAAAAAAAP!
WHOA, MAN, INDIGESTION SUCKS.
HE'S GETTING AWAY! MAYBE IF WE DOUBLE OUR EFFORTS AND RESTRAIN HIM, WE CAN THEN HACK HIM UP OR SOMETHING--
IT'S NO USE. WE CAN'T WIN.
I'M SO SORRY, SOFTBOY! THIS IS ALL MY FAULT, AND THE POWER OF FRIENDSHIP CAN'T FIX IT!
YOU WERE JUST TRYING TO GET YOUR FRIEND LAID, IT'S OKAY.
WAIT--
--OF COURSE!
MIAOW MIAOW! WE NEED MORE POWER TO CRUSH THE PARTY ANIMAL... SEXUAL POWER.
LIKE NOW?!
FINE, I'M ON IT.

HOW LONG DOES IT TAKE A GUY TO PEE...
SETH! WE NEED YOUR HELP!
JESUS, MIAOW MIAOW!
HEY, LOOK! IT'S A TALKING CAT.
ROCKSTAR AND SOFTBOY ARE THROWING EVERYTHING THEY'VE GOT AT THE PARTY ANIMAL, BUT IT'S NOT ENOUGH!
THEY NEED A POWER THAT'S EVEN STRONGER THAN FRIENDSHIP!
THEY NEED YOU.
UGH. FINE.
POWER BOTTOM POWER!
IT LOOKS LIKE YOU CAN HELP OUT, TOO.
HEHE.
BIG DICK ENERGY!

KNOWING ME--
--KNOWING YOU!
THERE IS NOTHING WE CAN'T DO!
BRA-ZHAAAAAAAM!
THAT NEEDED TO WORK, 'CUZ I CAN ALREADY FEEL MYSELF POWERING DOWN.
STUPID VISOR DOESN'T ACTUALLY DO ANYTHING TO ENHANCE MY VISION...

HE'S GONE, FOR REAL-REAL.
EVERYTHING CAN GO BACK TO NORMAL.
EVERYTHING-EVERYTHING? EVEN... US?
I LOVE YOU, SIS.
I'M EMOTIONALLY ROCK HARD RIGHT NOW.

TWO WEEKS LATER...

for Soft Boy
(and a little bit Rockstar)
OKAY, I KNOW IT'S A LITTLE PREMATURE, BUT...

...I THINK WE DESERVE A **TREAT.**
BUT I HAVEN'T LAUNCHED MY KICKSTARTER YET.
SURE, BUT PIVOTING FROM AN UNWIELDY VIDEO GAME TO A TABLETOP CARD GAME ABOUT THROWING THE PERFECT PARTY* DESERVES A GIFT IN AND OF ITSELF.
"PARTY ANIMAL", LAUNCHING NEXT QUARTER! --ED.
THAT'S REASON ENOUGH, THEN.
EVEN THOUGH WE DIDN'T GET SEMEN FLOWING, THAT PARTY CERTAINLY DID WONDERS FOR OUR **CREATIVE** JUICES!
MY NEW SONG **"QUTE"** IS GETTING A FINAL MIX TOMORROW!
OH MY **GOD!** FRIDA AND AGNETHA'S ICONIC CAT DRESSES!
THESE ARE **PERFECT.** I'M THINKING WE THROW THESE ON REAL QUICK AND...
...DANCE TO ABBA--
OH.
KIND OF ASSUMED THAT WAS A FOREGONE CONCLUSION.

AS WITH ANY ENDURING FRIENDSHIP, MORE CHALLENGES LAY AHEAD FOR THESE BFFS.
(INCLUDING A REALLY BIZARRE TRIP TO SPACE.)
NO MATTER WHEN AND WHERE THEIR STORY ENDS, HOWEVER, YOU CAN ALWAYS TRUST...
...ROCKSTAR AND SOFTBOY LIVED HAPPILY EVER AFTER.

The End

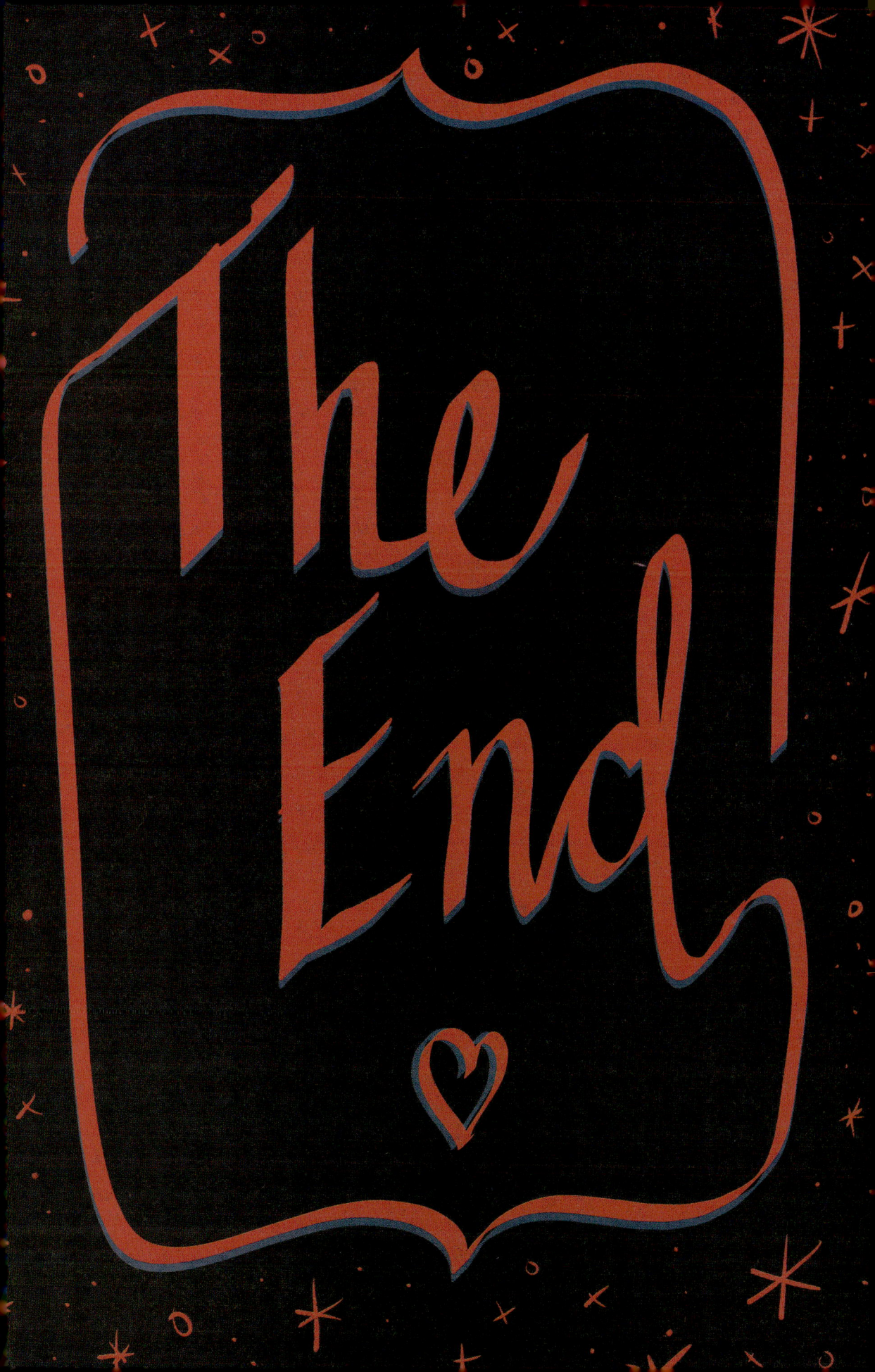

Hi, thank you for reading my comic.

As I sit here, looking over the final lettering for Rockstar and Softboy, I feel compelled to share some feelings I'm having about the whole process. The first feeling is that I'm grateful. The journey to date has brought me to a destination where I have the skills, the readership, and the support to tell a weird magical realist nonsensical story about gay bffs with one of the greatest mainstream publishers in comics. For a few years now, Eric Stephenson at Image Comics always encouraged me to pitch him ideas that I would write and draw. Jeff Boison would politely nudge me towards finding a story that had the charm of my autobio comics, but with a more universal, slightly high-concept approach. This is what I gave them: my response to there being a huge void for gay bff stories.

When I started telling my friends about this project, I kept saying "It's like Romy and Michele, or Broad City... but with zombies and sorcerers and gay guys instead of women." The more and more I pitched Rockstar and Softboy as that, the more depressed I got. For the better part of two decades, I've had to project my bff relationships onto female pairings in pop culture. This isn't necessarily a bad thing! Who doesn't appreciate having an argument over which best friend is the Mary and which one is the Rhoda-- so much fun! If you stop and really think about it, there aren't many iconic gay male-identifying pairings that persist in pop culture.

(Let's not get into Will and Jack of Will & Grace... I feel like those two tolerate each other more than actually appreciate and uplift one another.)

While I hope I've created something that oodles of people will appreciate, I must admit how much of the process involved me being ridiculously selfish in terms of making a product that reflects everything I desperately want to see in a comic book. That's why you have a protagonist who's hella balding, loves to talk about sex, and shrugs off gender conformity when throwing a look together. That's why I drew a super sentai magical girl transformation sequence where Rockstar and Softboy became something not quite power ranger, not quite sailor scout. Every page is an inside joke between me, myself, and I... that you paid nearly ten dollars to read.

This brings us to another feeling: Fun. Outside of the context that everyone is feeling through the years 2021 and 2022, I have gone through one of the most challenging and awful chapters of my life. I'm gonna leave it at "reasons untold and hardships unnumbered," but damn-- I've never been so beaten down by life's challenges! Including that one time I juggled a depressive era with a debilitating disorder in my esophagus! Everyone around me has been like, "Harness that pain and put it into a book."

To which I say, "Bitch. No."

I'm so sick of exploring and exploiting trauma for the sake of art. That's someone else's tea. Not mine (anymore). Everyone already knows queer people have it tough. Do people know why gay guys have super special friendships that would make even Lucy and Ethel jealous?

the hypothetical questions continue. Are readers getting enough reminders in their pop culture that life is so much more fun when you have a friend by your side who loves you in a near-codependent and totally platonic fashion, but is grown enough to butt out when a boundary is drawn? I can't tell you if this book has any deeper meaning, because my only goal in contributing to queer narratives is that I wanted to have fun honoring my friends.

No, but really the book is actually a meditation on intersectional families and generational trauma in post-colonial society, I swear.

Final feeling? I'm feeling good about my choices, y'all. I instinctively knew Rockstar and Softboy would work best under the parameters of being a one-shot. Even if there are more stories to tell with these characters, I knew the best way to debut them would be in a one-and-done package where they could have their adventure without the worry of diminishing returns, monthly deadlines, and book market forecasting. Sixty-four pages, what a fun size!

Thank you all, again, for letting me have some fun during a rough patch, creating one of the most fulfilling comics of my career.

Lots of love,

Sina Grace
January 2022

This is the tackiest photo I love it.

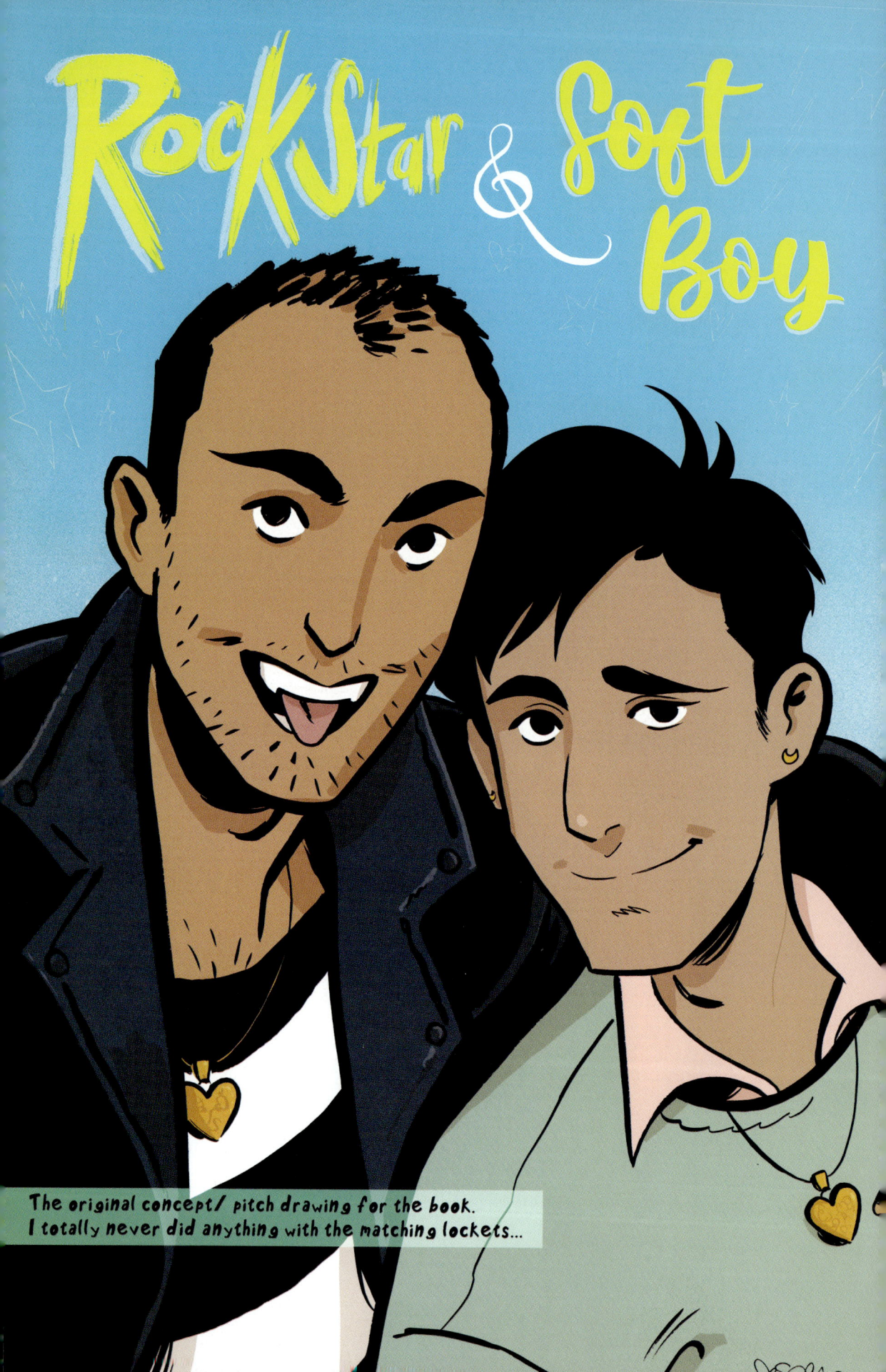

The original concept/pitch drawing for the book. I totally never did anything with the matching lockets...

What's in an origin story?

If you haven't guessed by now, this Rockstar and Softboy book you have in your hands is deeply inspired by my friendship with Josh Trujillo, and its creation came from both of us being losers.

Around the spring of 2021, Josh and I were competing on opposite sides of a bracket for DC Comics' Round Robin competition. Fans would vote on pitches us comic creators were developing, and the winner of the whole thing would in turn get a six-issue series greenlight. For the two months or whatever that Josh and I were in the competition, we chatted nearly every day for hours on end. We both made it to the final four (Josh with his splendid Blue Beetle idea and me with my killer Green Lanterns story), but after a particularly stressful voting window, we did not make it to the final two. As Josh and I were commiserating, he mentioned giving the winning writer on his side of the bracket a call to congratulate him. My response was something like, "fuck that, I'm not congratulating T** S*****! I'm pissed as shit!"

Josh quietly replied with, "well that's because you're the Rockstar and I'm the Softboy."

Right then and there, I knew we weren't going to walk away from the competition as losers. Rockstar and Softboy was the title of a comic... a winner of a comic, at that! I told Eric Stephenson the whole story, how I wanted to make a book that was a celebration of two gay best friends coming together to stop a Party Animal, and he was gracious enough to let Image Comics be the home for this project.

While I spouted a bunch of very true words about how this book is a product of love and fun, I need to make it abundantly clear: a lot of ideas need the fuel of spite to actually hit the finish line. You're reading a book about two creative gays in a magical world sticking together through thick and thin because I was an incredibly sore loser.

So, if you find yourself in a particularly petty state of mind when you're writing or drawing, and there's that "I'll show so-and-so" voice going off in the back of your head... run with it. Indulge that anger and harness it into creating something totally undeniable.

Just make sure your good friends check in on you and keep the pettiness from fully reigning supreme.

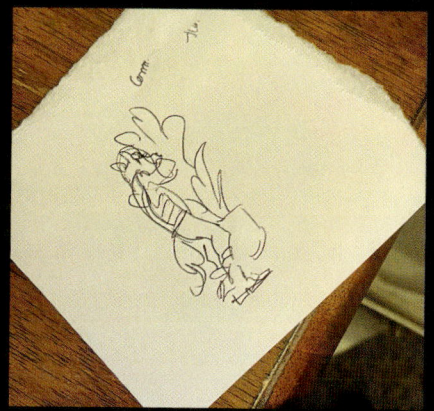

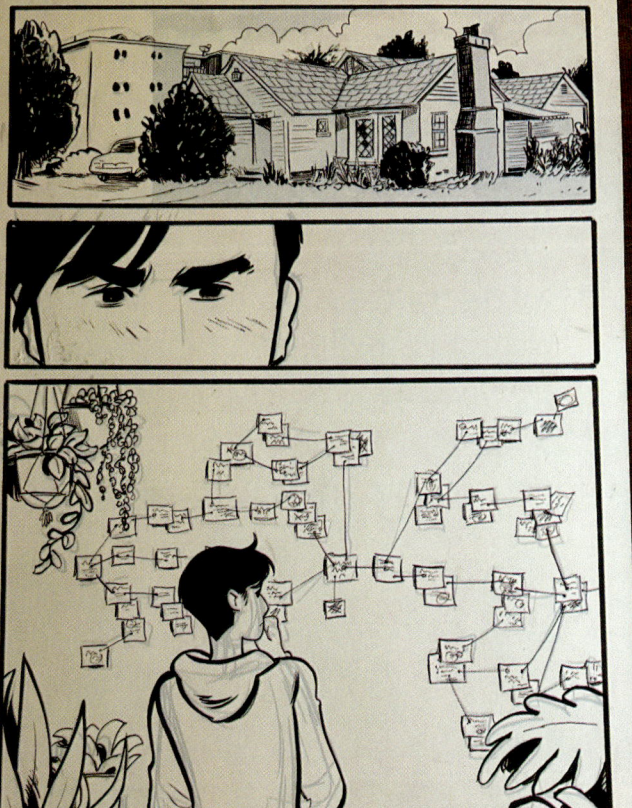

While I always had a clear sense of the story for Rockstar and Softboy, landing the style for art took a minute to figure out!

Take a glance at some of the original pages I drew before sorting out my final art style!

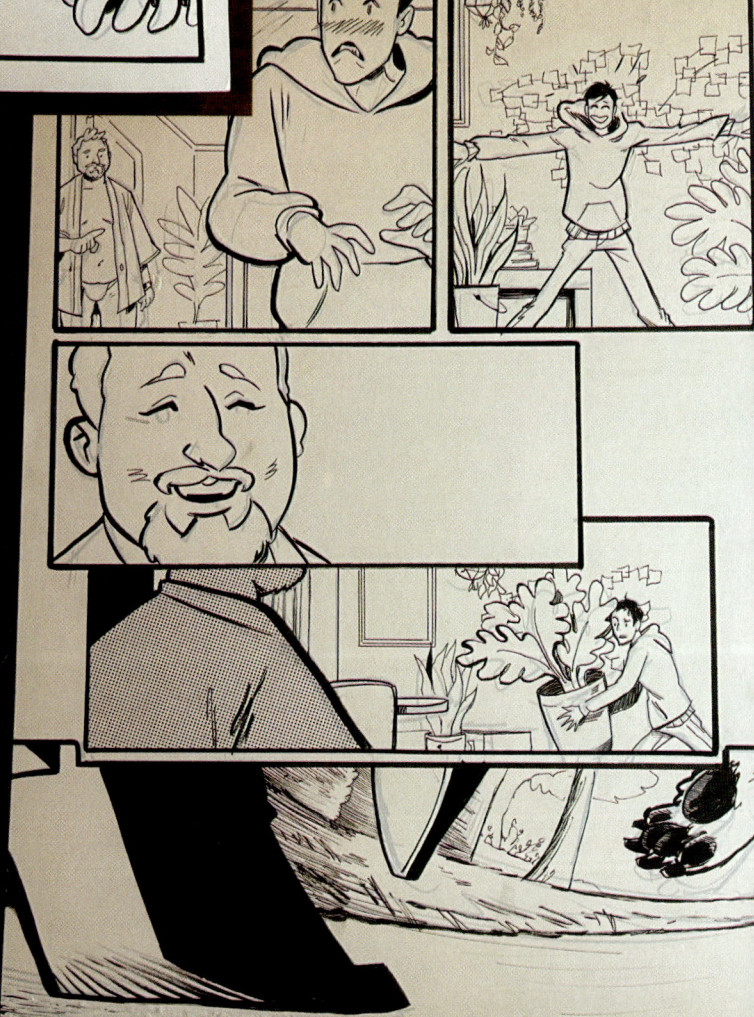

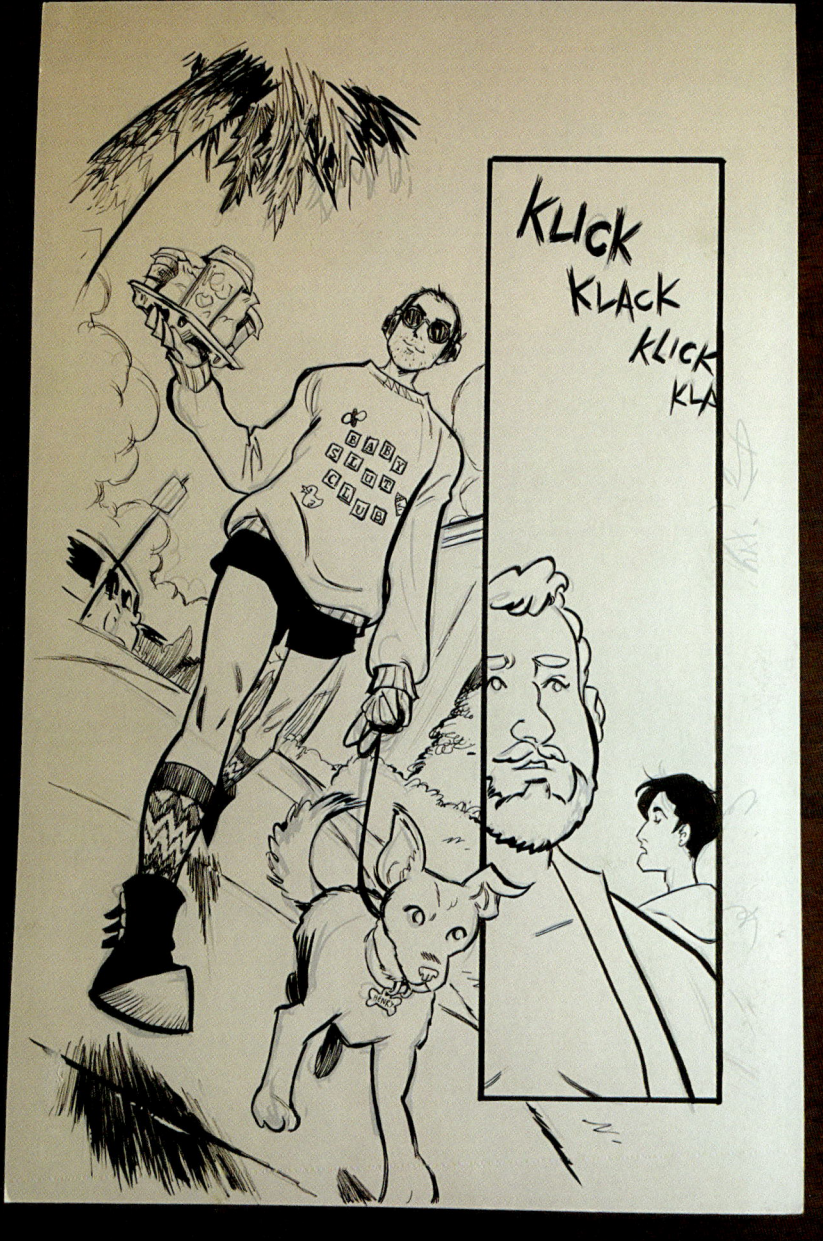

I still feel bad that I opted to take my dog Henry out of the book but a cat who morphs into a chain smoking woman was animal enough

PART ANIMAL...
...PART...
PARTY ANIMAL!
still getting the hang of figuring
how to draw these characters...
its own feels like the way to go...
6/7/21

FROM THERE, THE PAIR BECAME INSEPARABLE. BOUNCING IDEAS OFF ONE-ANOTHER, EMBRACING THEIR DIFFERENCES,
FINDING NEW

It was a struggle to trust how the characters wanted to be drawn... I resisted my instincts and kept trying to find a Jamie Hewlett/Jillian Tamaki fusion way to draw.

lookit the original version of the last page! the line weights are wonky, proportions stupid, and the art just looks scratchy and unsure of itself. Bless the power of deadlines and me loving the final art style!

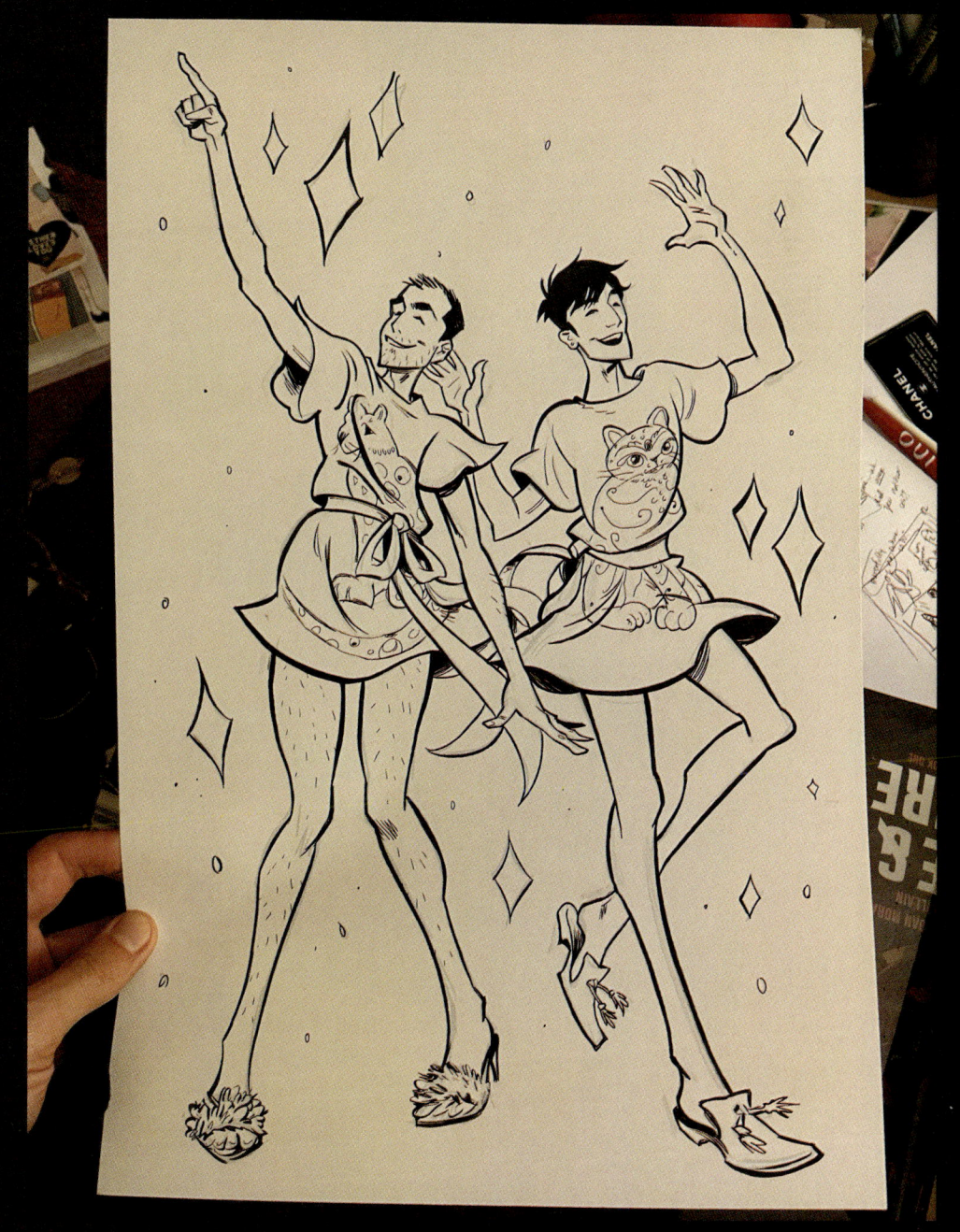

Are you a fan of writer/babe...
...JOSH TRUJILLO?
TAYLOR SWIFT
ABBA

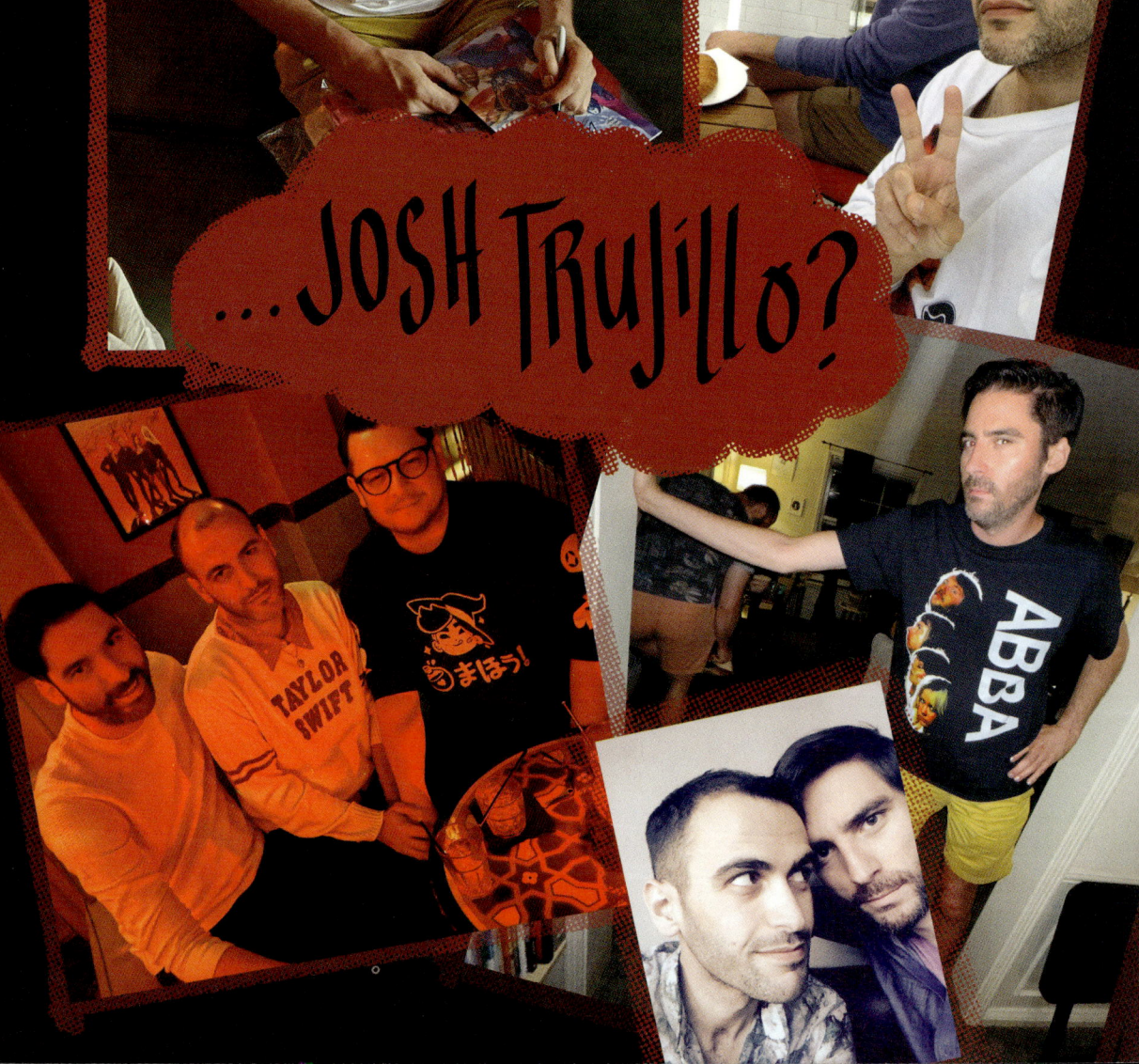

Party Game Idea...
"BORT SOMPSON"

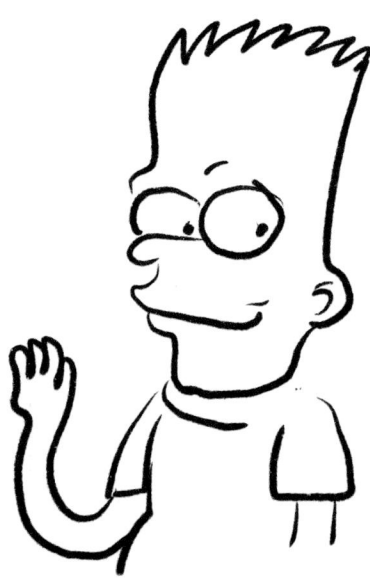

The concept:
Without any reference, folks must draw Bart Simpson from memory! Results are 100% hilarious and great. Talent and budget not necessary!

The rules:
Give contestants like 2 minutes to draw "Bort Sompson" on a sheet of printer paper.

The prize:
Funniest Bort gets your Disney+ login.

special thx to Becky Cloonan for showing me this game :)

SPECIAL THX

- Mikael aka Mikaekae aka Miketto aka Kethry614
- Mom
- Little Jackebrownes Brayden + Sean
- Isabell Ivy
- Anthony Foster? (delivered)
- Nick Dinosaurio
- Jason Aloise
- #1 Bish Steven Canals
- Eric Stephenson (mark)
- Audrey & Aki (corbo)
- Harris Miller
- Meet Trish Behind The Mall!
- Robert Motherlode Cute
- Desmona Maré
- Dyl Nas X
- The "J Crew" → Charlotte, Zani & Helen
- Matthew Herman
- Spendrina
- Daniel Freedman
- Ian O'Phelan
- East Side Book Club
- Buk Kloob
- Chris Robinson

Do You Know the fucking VIBES!?

It takes more than ABBA & friendship to keep me drawing..

COLLEEN GREEN
COOL

Process: lighting a good candle

Candy: Sour Patch Kids, Twizzlers

Hakuna Matata

Social media: memes + inside jokes with ppl I've never met IRL

Well if this ain't a #mood:
Hahahahahahahahahahahaha
The ducking vibes
Very that

Boy
Smells

Pets!! Henry, Otis, Amelia (RIP), Sally, Hauke, Mimi, Gray

CAFFEINE!

Music: Caleb Nichols
Peach Kelli Pop
Riki
Doja Cat
Hunx & His Punx
Vivian Girls
Colleen Green
TRST
Beck
Lil Nas X
old Blink 182
Health
Feels
etc etc etc

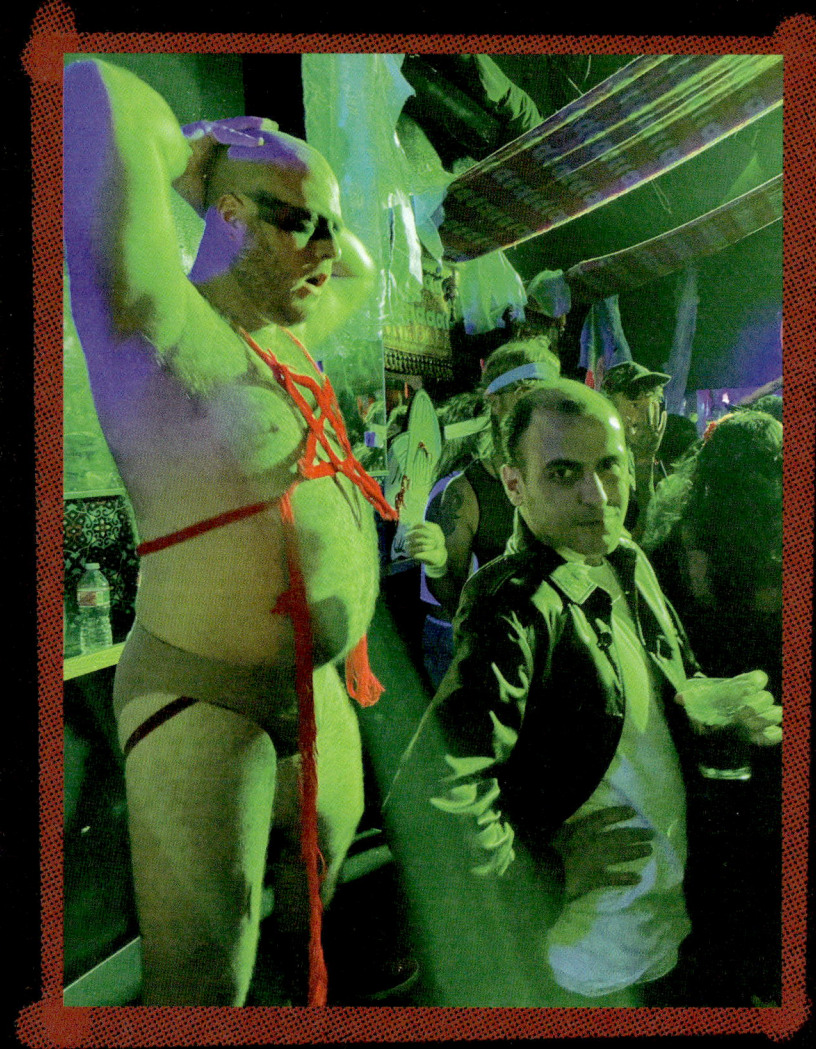

About the Author

Sina Grace is a writer and illustrator lowkey thriving in Los Angeles, CA. He got his start at Image Comics drawing The Li'l Depressed Boy, and made a home there with his slice-of-life memoir (Self-Obsessed, Nothing Lasts Forever). People mostly know him from slaying on Iceman at Marvel Comics and doing art for his fave musician, Jenny Lewis. He loves his friends... a lot.

@sinagrace everywhere * sinagrace..com